THOMAS & FRIENDS™

ANNUAL 2001

Contents

Britt Allcroft's Thomas the Tank Engine & Friends
Based on The Railway Series by The Rev W Awdry © Britt Allcroft (Thomas) LLC 2000
All underlying rights worldwide Britt Allcroft (Thomas) LLC

THOMAS THE TANK ENGINE & FRIENDS and THOMAS & FRIENDS are trademarks of Britt Allcroft Inc
in the USA, Mexico and Canada and of Britt Allcroft (Thomas) Limited in the rest of the world.
THE BRITT ALLCROFT COMPANY is a trademark of The Britt Allcroft Company plc

Published in Great Britain in 2000 by Egmont World Limited,
a division of Egmont Holding Limited,
Deanway Technology Centre, Wilmslow Road, Handforth, Cheshire SK9 3FB
Printed in Italy   ISBN 0 7498 4861 8

Very Special Engines

Lots of people visit the island of Sodor each year. Some of them come for the day, and some of them stay for a longer holiday. The people who live on Sodor are proud of their little island, and they like to share it with as many visitors as possible.

Holiday posters show people what the island is like. This year a famous photographer called Paul Carter came to the island to take some new photographs. The best one was going to be chosen to be on a new poster.

Sir Topham Hatt, The Fat Controller, is very proud of the island. He is even more proud of his railway and his very special engines.

When he heard that Mr Carter would be coming by train, he made sure that he got a special welcome at the Big Station.

Thomas the Tank Engine and his friends are also proud of the island. Their job was to take Mr Carter to all sorts of different places on the island. Bertie the bus helped, too.

Mr Carter found lots of interesting things on Sodor, and he took lots and lots of photographs. Sir Topham Hatt and the mayor were going to help him choose the best one.

There were lots of photos to look at. There was a picture of cows and sheep in the fields by the side of Thomas' branch line, and a picture that was taken at the seashore very early in the morning, when the boats came into the harbour with the fish they had caught. There were pictures of the beach and the mountains, and busy scenes at the Big Station.

"It's going to be very difficult to choose just one photograph," said The Fat Controller. "There are such a lot of lovely places on the island."

The mayor nodded his head. "Yes," he said. "What we have to find is the one special picture that will show people what a special place Sodor is, and make them want to come here for a visit or a holiday."

The Fat Controller, the mayor and Mr Carter chose their favouite pictures and spread them out on the table. "Now, how can we choose just one of them?" asked the mayor.

Mr Carter smiled. "I think I know," he said. "Look at the pictures. There is one special thing in each one of them."

Sir Topham looked at the pictures very carefully. "Yes!" he said. "It's the engines! There's one of my railway engines in each picture! Look, there's Thomas on his branch line, Henry and the Flying Kipper collecting the fish from the harbour, and James chuffing along on the line at the back of the beach. There's Gordon the express steaming into the Big Station to pick up his passengers, and Edward working hard on the steep little mountain line."

The mayor nodded. "I think we've found one of the things that make the island so special – your railway, Sir Topham."

"And my friendly engines, of course," said Sir Topham. "Everyone who comes to the island likes to see them. They bring a smile to every boy's and girl's face. Thomas and his friends really are Very Special Engines."

Mr Carter put the photographs away and got out his camera. "I'd like to take one more photograph at the Big Station. Can you arrange for Thomas and the engines to be there, Sir Topham?"

Thomas and his friends were very pleased and proud to be in the special photograph. When Mr Carter said, "Smile, please!" they all smiled an extra big smile.

"Peep, peep!" said Thomas.

Come to SODOR and meet these Very Special Engines!

Smile, Please!

Paul Carter took lots and lots of photographs of Thomas and his friends.

Look carefully.

Which two pictures of **Thomas** are exactly the **same**?

Which picture of **Percy** is **different**?

a

b

d

c

e

f

g

h

i

13

Thomas the Famous Engine

Diesel isn't very popular in the yard. He enjoys being mean and causing trouble.

2. "He's always playing nasty tricks on us," said Percy. "He really gets up my funnel!"

3. One day Diesel buzzed into the yard. "I've got a message for you, Thomas," he said.

4. "The Fat Controller says you must wait for a crate to be loaded before you go to your branch line."

5. Thomas waited and waited, but no crate came. Diesel sniggered. There was no crate. It was a fib!

6. Thomas was very late, which he didn't like at all. "The men will be late for work at the quarry!" he said.

7. But Diesel didn't care. He thought it was such a great joke that he decided to try it on Gordon.

8. Gordon waited, then he had to steam at top speed to get to the Big Station, hissing and puffing hard.

9. "Where have you been?" said The Fat Controller. "You shouldn't keep passengers waiting. Now hurry!"

10. Duck doesn't like Diesel. He once got him into trouble for something he didn't do.

11. "Diesel is very mean to all of us," said Duck. "I think he needs to be taught a lesson."

12. When Diesel came into the yard later, he saw Duck trying to get a row of trucks on to a siding.

13. Diesel laughed. "You don't know anything about moving trucks! I can move them easily! I'll show you!"

14. Diesel purred up to the trucks. He didn't know that they were very old and rusty Troublesome Trucks.

15. Their brakes were stiff, and their wheels needed oiling. They were VERY hard to move around.

16. Diesel struggled, banging and crashing them along. He roared with anger. "Move, you silly trucks!"

17. Diesel pulled as hard as he could, and a coupling broke, SNAP! He shot forward very fast indeed.

18. Then Diesel moved back and banged into the trucks as hard as he could.
It made them screech and clang.

19. Just then, along came The Fat Controller. "Now that's not the way to move trucks, Diesel," he said.

20. "Don't be so rough with them. Why don't you let Duck show you how it should be done?"

21. Duck moved the trucks slowly and gently. Diesel had to stand and watch and sulk. He felt very silly.

22. That night, Duck told the other engines what had happened. Thomas and Gordon were very pleased.

23. "So Diesel looked silly for a change, did he?" said Gordon. "I'm glad. It's about time."

24. "Serves him right!" said Thomas. "I bet he doesn't think his tricks are so funny now. Well done, Duck!"

Read with Thomas

Read this story yourself. There are pictures in place of some of the words to help you.

Toby the Tram Engine works on the

 that goes to the  . He works

with his coach who is called Henrietta. They

are both painted brown. They take

all the  to work and pull big

 full of  .

A young  works on the line, too.

Her name is Mavis.

One day the  were very full and

there were lots of them.

"I can take them on my own!" said  .

"Oh no, you can't!" said  . "They

are too heavy for  engine to pull."

"Toby is right," said  . "Take

the trucks in two lots. Take some to the

 then come back for the

others." Mavis was angry with  .

"You have got some silly ideas," she said.

Mavis was angry with  too.

"You don't know anything about

 ," she said. "You were

going to be made into a

for  to live in when you were

rescued by  ."

Mavis set off with all the  .

But they were so heavy that she had to

stop at the  .

Mavis waited and waited.

She was very pleased when she heard

Toby's big . Ring, ding, ding!

 and Henrietta helped .

Working as a team they got the trucks moving again, and  said how sorry she was. "I have a lot to learn from both of you. You aren't the newest engine, . And , you look a bit odd but you are both Really Useful!" Toby was so pleased that he rang his  again.

Ring, ding, ding!

The Good Old Days

Duke is the oldest of the narrow-gauge railway engines. He's good and kind, and likes to help the younger engines by giving them advice. He keeps them in their place, too, but in a very kind way.

Thomas always stops for a chat when he sees Duke. He likes to hear his stories about what the railway used to be like when Duke was new. Duke calls those times The Good Old Days.

One day, Duke was telling Thomas about when he used to pull very heavy quarry wagons.

When Gordon the big express chuffed past at top speed, Thomas said, "Peep, peep! Hello, Fat face!"

"**Really, Thomas!**" said Duke. "You shouldn't talk to a senior engine like that. In my day, the younger engines weren't as cheeky as you are. They knew their place. The work we did was very hard, and we didn't have time for fun and mischief, not like you youngsters today. There were rules for everything, and we all had to obey them. We had to work together and help each other. And we had to do just as we were told – or else!"

"Peep!" said Thomas. "I don't like the sound of that! It sounds like The BAD Old Days! I think it's better now, without so many rules and things. I do work VERY hard on my branch line, you know, Duke, and I'm never, never late. But I like to have some fun, too!"

"You can have fun without being cheeky," said Duke. "I'm going to have some fun on Sunday. I'm going to pull the special picnic train up to the lake. The summer visitors love it. Pip! I know all the very best places for picnics!"

"Phew!" said Thomas. "It's a tough run up to the lake, Duke, uphill all the way. The track is very steep. Will you manage it?"

"Peep, pip, peep! Of course I will!" said Duke. "I may be getting old, young Thomas, but I've still got plenty of steam in my boiler! I can still show you young engines a thing or two about pulling trains!"

When Thomas steamed into the yard on Saturday afternoon he was surprised to see Duke standing in the repair shed. "Hello, Duke," he said. "Is something wrong?"

Duke looked very sad and sorry for himself. "It's my old valves, Thomas," he said. "They're leaking, and the steam is escaping."

"Don't worry," said Thomas. "The men will mend you. You'll be as good as new in a day or so."

"I know," said Duke. "But I won't be able to pull the picnic train tomorrow."

"Peep! I'd pull it for you," said Thomas. "But I can't pull trains on the narrow-gauge lines."

"It's very kind of you," said Duke. "But if you pulled my train it would break the rules, too. It's not allowed. It's my job to pull the picnic train. The trip will have to be cancelled."

"But think how disappointed the visitors will be when they can't go for a picnic," said Thomas. "Can't we change the rules, just this once? There must be another engine who could help."

Duke smiled. "Well, perhaps we can break the rules just this once, as long as you find a reliable, sensible engine to take over, Thomas," he said. "I won't let just any engine pull my train."

"**Rheneas** would look after the passengers well," said Thomas. "But he breaks down a lot.

Duncan could do the job, but he thinks he does too much work already.

Sir Handel learned a lot from you, Duke, but he can be bad-tempered."

Thomas thought hard.

"Peep!" he said. "I've got it! Peter Sam can pull the picnic train. I know he teases you about being old, Duke, but he thinks you're a fine old engine really. He's happy and kind, and he works hard and never ever grumbles. He's just the engine we need!"

Peter Sam was glad to help. He made a very good job of pulling the picnic train up to the lake.

When he got back, Duke and Thomas were waiting for him outside the repair shed. "I've got new valves," Duke told Peter Sam. "I'm as good as new again. Thank you for pulling my train."

"I was pleased to help," said Peter Sam.

"Thank you for your help, too, Thomas," said Duke.

"It was nothing," said Thomas.

Duke smiled. "You two young engines have shown how we should all work together and help each other," said Duke. "It's great, just like **The Good Old Days!**"

The Picnic Race

Sir Handel is an old engine who thinks he knows everything. One day he and his friend Duncan had a race to see who knew the quickest way to Duke's favourite picnic place.

Play the game with a friend. You need a die and a counter each. One of you is Sir Handel and the other is Duncan.

Take turns to roll the die.
Move the number on the die. If you roll 3, move 3 places, and so on.

If you land on ...

move UP

move DOWN

have an extra throw

miss a turn

go back 2

Who will win the picnic race?

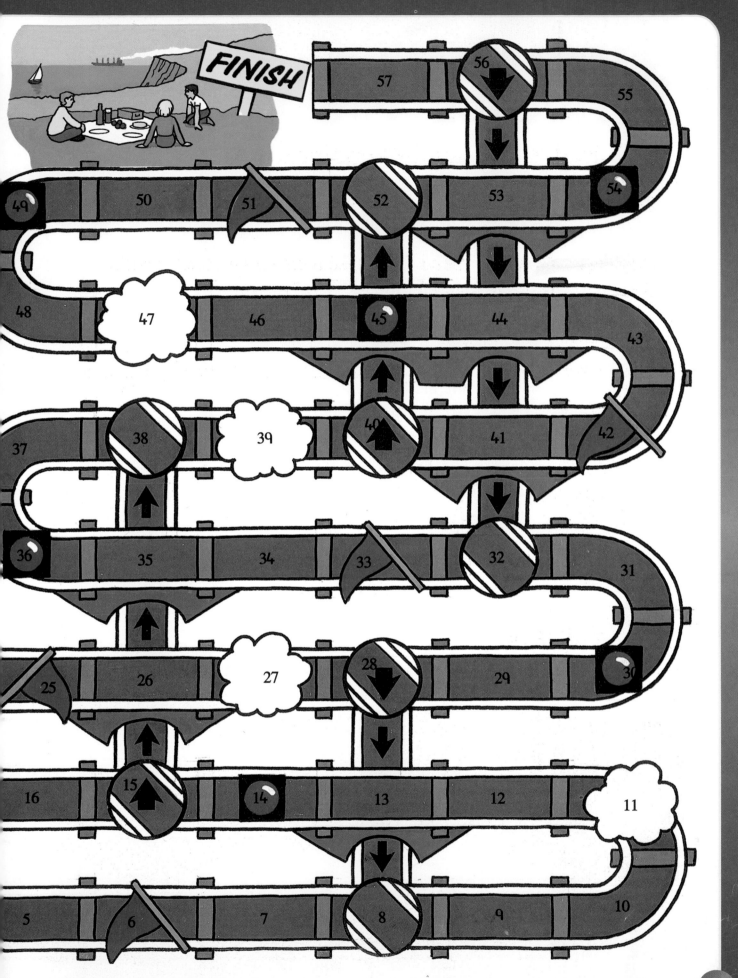

THOMAS & FRIENDS™

COMPETITION TIME!

We've got some very special prizes for our Thomas readers, courtesy of Racing Champions, whose super products are made to the very highest standards. These beautiful toys are authentic in every detail!

30 THOMAS PRIZES TO BE WON!

We have six Thomas and Friends Starter Sets containing 8 pieces of track, a Thomas die-cast Engine, Annie and Clarabel

plus

24 very special, limited edition Millennium Thomas Engines – a real collector's item that you'll treasure for years to come.

HOW TO ENTER

All you have to do is unscramble these letters to spell out the name of a famous Thomas and Friends character:

HET TAF LORNTRELOC

Write your answer on a postcard or on the back of a sealed envelope (don't forget to put your name, address and age), and post it to: THOMAS & FRIENDS ANNUAL COMPETITION, EGMONT WORLD LIMITED, DEANWAY TECHNOLOGY CENTRE, WILMSLOW ROAD, HANDFORTH, CHESHIRE SK9 3FB

RULES
1. 30 winners will be chosen at random and notified by post.
2. Judges' decision will be final. No correspondence will be entered into.
3. The winners' names will be made available from Egmont World Limited (on request) after 5th February 2001. Please enclose a stamped addressed envelope for reply.
4. Employees (and their relatives) of Egmont World Limited and their associated companies are not eligible to enter.
5. Entries are limited to one per person.
6. Competition is open to residents of the UK, Channel Islands, and Ireland only.
7. The Publishers reserve the right to vary prizes, subject to availability.
8. Closing date for entries is 26th January 2001.

Edward Saves the Day

Henry, the big green number 3 engine, is very fast and powerful. He likes everything he does to be just right, but sometimes he worries about things so much that it makes him ill.

Summer was a very busy time for Henry. There were lots of visitors to take all over the island, and he had to pull the Flying Kipper from the harbour every morning, loaded with fish. Henry worked very hard, and it all got a bit too much. Things started to go wrong with him.

"**Henry has been working** too hard," said The Fat Controller. "It's made him ill. He must go away to be repaired, and have a long rest."

But sending Henry away left Sir Topham with a problem. Which engine would do Henry's work?

Sir Topham tried Gordon, the fastest and most powerful engine. Gordon tried to help, but he had to do his own job as well, pulling the big express, and after a few days he got very tired.

Cheeky, fussy Thomas was very eager to help. But he's a small engine, and after a day of trying to do Henry's work as well as the work on his own branch line, even he had to admit that it was too much for him. "I'm sorry, Sir Topham," said Thomas. "I did try very hard."

"I know you did, Thomas," said Sir Topham. "And I'm very grateful, but another engine will have to do Henry's work tomorrow." Sir Topham looked around. "What about you, James? Can you help?"

But James did not like the idea of working so hard. He thought his fine red paint and shiny brass dome might get dirty. "I don't think I can do Henry's work as well as my own," he said. "I am a Really Splendid Engine, after all!"

Like Thomas, Percy the junior engine wanted to help. "But you have more than enough work to do in the yard, keeping all the trucks in order," said Sir Topham. "It's very important work, and I just can't spare you, Percy."

Everyone wondered what would happen. Who would do Henry's work until he came back?

Thomas fussed around. "Peep, peep! We've got to think of something! We've got to think of something!" he said.

Gordon fretted and worried, and Percy tried to think of some way that he could help. Even James looked a little bit worried.

The engines were in a bit of a panic – all except Edward, the old blue number 2 engine. He didn't make a fuss or waste time rushing around. No, Edward just took charge of things, in his usual calm and kind way.

"Gordon, you pull the express, as usual," he said. "Thomas, you go to your branch line, because that's where you're needed. Percy, you carry on doing your good work with the trucks – and James, you just carry on being a Really Splendid Engine, because it's what you do best."

Then Edward spoke to Sir Topham. "The other engines must all carry on with their own jobs," he said quietly. "And I will take over from Henry."

The Fat Controller smiled. "Right, Edward," he said. "I knew I could rely on you to calm everyone down and get things sorted out. Thank you, Edward, and off you go."

Edward did Henry's work without making any fuss. It was hard work, but he enjoyed it.

At the end of the week, Sir Topham went to the shed to speak to the engines. "I've got some good news," he said. "Henry is working well again, and will soon be back. Until then, I know I can rely on all of you to help keep the railway running well. I have to thank Edward most of all. He's not as fast as Henry or as powerful as Gordon," he said. "He's not as handsome as James, and not as good with the trucks as Percy. But this week Edward has proved that he is a Really Useful Engine."

Thomas blew some steam out of his funnel. "What about me?" he said. "You didn't talk about me."

Sir Topham smiled. "And Edward is not as **cheeky** as you, Thomas!" he said.

"Peep, peep!" said Thomas.

THOMAS
AND THE MAGIC RAILROAD ™

Thomas and the Magic Railroad is a romantic comedy action adventure packed with thrills, spills, whistles and steam. It is a story about trains, people who lived far apart and a railroad that brought them together.

A family film for all ages, the film chronicles the adventures of ten-year-old Lily who sets off to visit her lonely Grandpa, but finds herself on a great adventure along the way that leads to a meeting with the world's favourite steam engine: Thomas the Tank Engine.

In a classic good-versus-evil story, Lily's and Thomas' harmonious world of magic and innocence are put in jeopardy by greed and cynicism. Lily, along with a host of other colourful characters, triumphs and brings the story to its happy end.

Britt Allcroft, creator, producer and director of **Thomas and the Magic Railroad.**

New Characters

Diesel 10

A renegade diesel engine on the Island of Sodor who gets 10 out of 10 for brutal strength and devious deeds and who is out to destroy the harmony of Sir Topham Hatt's railway.

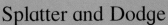

Lady

A very special golden engine, who holds the secret to the Magic Railroad.

Splatter and Dodge

Splatter, left, and his twin, Dodge, are Diesel 10's silly sidekicks. They plot and scheme, but are not really quite as tough as they would like to think they are.

Behind the Scenes

The Shining Time Station main building.

Mr Conductor's magical mural inside the Shining Time Station.

Filming the outside sequences in the Isle of Man countryside.

Didi Conn (Stacy Jones), Mara Wilson (Lily) and the crew filming outside Shining Time Station.

Make a Thomas Jigsaw

Have fun making this Thomas jigsaw.

You need:

- a postcard or piece of card
- pencil
- ruler
- felt-tip pens
- safety scissors

1.Draw 3 lines to divide the postcard into 6 parts, like this:

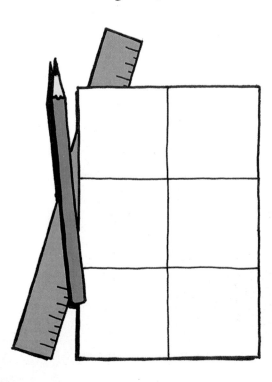

2.Copy Thomas on to the card section by section.

3. Colour the picture and cut into 6 pieces.
Cut along the lines.

4. Mix up the jigsaw pieces.
Can you fit them back together again?

Best Friends

Thomas and Bertie the Bus are the best of friends. But it was not always like that.

One day, Thomas was working hard on his branch line. He was waiting for Henry's train, which was coming from the main line.

But Henry was late, and Thomas was not pleased. "How can I run my branch line properly if I have to wait around like this?" he said. "**I'M** never late!"

Bertie the Bus was waiting for Henry, too. He was going to take some of the passengers home.

Thomas and Bertie had a chat and told stories to help pass the time while they waited. "Do you remember the first time I took some of your passengers for you?" asked Bertie, smiling.

"Oh, yes," said Thomas. "I wasn't very pleased, was I? Mind you, I didn't know how useful buses were then."

"That's right," said Bertie. "You wanted to do everything yourself, without any help from a silly old bus like me. You said you were faster than me, and I said you weren't. We argued. We couldn't agree on who was fastest."

"So we had a race to settle it," said Thomas.

"And I was soon in the lead," said Bertie.

"Peep!" said Thomas. "Oh yes, I remember that! You set off very fast while I was getting up speed. But then you had to wait at the gate at the level crossing, and I sped through!"

"I soon caught up with you again, though," said Bertie. "And by the time we got to the bridge, I was out in front."

"That's right," said Thomas. "My coaches, Annie and Clarabel, were very worried about me. I had to stop at the station for a big, long drink of water, then I got up a lot of steam and chuffed off after you at top speed. Do you remember, Bertie, how I called out to you as you were waiting at a red traffic light?"

"Yes, you called me slowcoach!" said Bertie. "It took a long time for the lights to turn to green. I was stuck there for ages. But by the time I got to where the road and the railway track ran side by side, I had nearly caught up with you. Our passengers were all cheering us on. They were enjoying themselves as much as we were."

"Yes," said Thomas. "I thought you were going to catch me again, so I put on a little bit of extra speed, and I managed to stay ahead. Then when you had to climb the big hill, I took the short way through the long tunnel. I rushed through as fast as I could, and chuffed into the station just as you came down the hill. I was puffed out, I can tell you."

Bertie smiled. "Yes, so was I. But you won the race, Thomas," he said.

"The other engines still talk about it in the shed sometimes," said Thomas. "They call it The Great Race."

Thomas and Bertie were having a good time talking about their famous race. They were having such a good time that they didn't hear Henry arriving until he blew his whistle extra-loud. It surprised them and made them jump.

Henry was impatient because he was late. "Are you two going to sit there chatting all day?" he said. "There's work to be done, you know! You two are going to make us all late!"

Thomas looked at Bertie.

Bertie looked at Thomas.

"Late indeed!" said Bertie.

"Well!" said Thomas. "Peep, peep! What a cheek!"

Bertie smiled. "Toot, toot!"

The Great Race

Thomas and Bertie want to have another race, but The Fat Controller won't let them. So they play this race game instead. You can play, too.

You need a die and two counters, one for Thomas and one for Bertie. You can play on your own, or with a friend.
Roll the die. Move Thomas along the track and move Bertie along the road.
If you land on a picture, you must do what it tells you.

START

Signs for Thomas

miss a turn   throw again   go on 3   go back 3   go on 1   go back 4

Signs for Bertie

miss a turn **throw again** **go back 3** **go on 3** **go back 1** **go on 2**

Donald and Douglas

It was winter on the island of Sodor, and everything was covered in a blanket of thick snow.

2. The snow looked nice, and the children loved it, but it made things very hard for the engines.

3. The engines often teased old Terence the tractor about having funny tracks instead of wheels.

4. But when it snowed they were glad to see him. "You can pull us out if we get stuck!" said Percy.

5. **Thomas agreed.** "When I started work on my branch line, I got stuck and Terence pulled me out."

6. **Later that day** the snow was still falling when Sir Topham Hatt, The Fat Controller, had some bad news.

7. "**Stepney is stuck** in a snowdrift near the harbour. He's too far away for Terence to reach him quickly."

8. "**But Stepney** must be moved, or the Main Line will be blocked," Sir Topham told the engines.

9. Sir Topham sent Donald and Douglas, the Scottish twin tender engines, to rescue Stepney.

10. The twins are very good at ploughing snow, and they steamed off as fast as they could go.

11. Their big front snowploughs made showers of snow that piled up on the sides of the track.

12. Stepney was pleased to see Donald and Douglas. He was glad to see the men, too.

13. **The men** used their shovels to clear the snow away from Stepney. Soon they were all back in the yard.

14. **The Fat Controller** was pleased. "Well done, Donald and Douglas," he said. "Take the rest of the day off."

15. **Sir Topham** took the men into his office. "You deserve a nice hot drink," he told them.

16. **Donald** and Douglas still had their snowploughs on, and decided to have some fun with them.

17. **Stepney** watched them chuffing around the yard. They piled up the snow and pushed it around gently.

18. **When** The Fat Controller came out of his office again, there was a big surprise waiting for him!

19. **Standing** by the side of the track was a snowman. It was big and round and had black coal eyes!

20. **The snowman** looked just like The Fat Controller! "It's Sir Topham Snowman!" said Stepney.

21. Sir Topham smiled. "I like your snowman very much," he said. "Which one of you made it?"

22. "It was Donald!" said Douglas. "No it wasn't," said Donald. "It was my brother Douglas!"

23. The Fat Controller turned to ask Stepney – but he wasn't going to say who it was, either!

24. "Never mind," said Sir Topham, and he took off his black top hat and put it on the snowman's head!

Count with Donald and Douglas

Donald and Douglas had lots of fun making their Fat Controller snowman!

**Find these things in the big picture and count them.
Write a number for each one.**

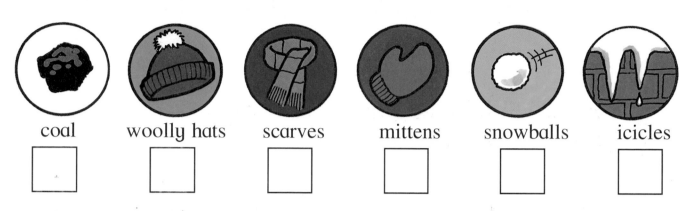

coal	woolly hats	scarves	mittens	snowballs	icicles
☐	☐	☐	☐	☐	☐

Read with Thomas

R ead this story yourself.
There are little pictures in place of some words to help you.

It was  time, and it was

going to be a big day for  .

A very important visitor was coming to the

 . Lots of  were

coming to meet him, and Thomas was pleased

when  asked  to bring him.

That night in the shed Thomas felt very excited.

"Take it easy," said  , but Thomas said, "I just can't wait!"

"I remember when being impatient got

you into big trouble," said  .

"So do I," said  .

"And I remember as well!" said Thomas.

When Thomas fell asleep he had a  ...

When  was ill, Thomas pulled a

 for the first time. But he could

not wait, and set off without his

and his  !

He took no notice of the  who tried to stop him. He only stopped when a

 told him to go back. The

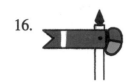, the station master and the

were angry with him! Poor  !

When Thomas woke up in the morning he

told  and  that he

had learned a lesson from the dream. "I'm not

going to be impatient again. I promise!"

At  , lots of  came to

the Big Station.

Thomas chuffed in with his visitor.

The Fat Controller opened the  and out

stepped  ! He had a great big

full of  . There was one for every

 and every .The  was

pleased with Thomas, and let him turn on

the Christmas 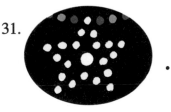 .

 was so happy that he forgot his

promise not to get excited, and he made an

extra loud, "Peep, PEEP!"